DETROIT PUBLIC LIBRARY

P9-EEU-543

CHASE BRANCH LIBRARY
17731 W. SEVEN MILE RD.
DETROIT, MI 48235

CH

For Anne and Mabel
— J.G.

To the fans of the wily red cat!
— N.R.

The character of Rotten Ralph was originally created by
Jack Gantos and Nicole Rubel.
Copyright © 2009 by John B. Gantos, Jr.
Copyright © 2009 by Nicole Rubel

All rights reserved. For information about permission to
reproduce selections from this book, write to
Permissions, Houghton Mifflin Company,
215 Park Avenue South, New York, New York 10003.

Houghton Mifflin Books for Children is an imprint of
Houghton Mifflin Harcourt Publishing Company.

www.hmhbooks.com

Library of Congress Cataloging Publication Data
Gantos, Jack.
The nine lives of Rotten Ralph / written by Jack Gantos;
illustrated by Nicole Rubel.
p. cm.
Summary: When the veterinarian determines that Sarah's cat has used up
eight of his nine lives, will the high-spirited feline finally stop misbehaving?
ISBN 978-0-618-80046-9
[1. Cats—Fiction. 2. Behavior—Fiction.] I. Rubel, Nicole, ill. II. Title.
PZ7.G15334Ni 2009
[E]—dc22
2008033878

Manufactured in China
CAC 10 9 8 7 6 5 4 3 2 1

The Nine Lives
of Rotten Ralph

Written by **Jack Gantos**

Illustrated by **Nicole Rubel**

Houghton Mifflin Books for Children

Houghton Mifflin Harcourt • Boston 2009

Rotten Ralph loved being Sarah's cat.
He lived a charmed life doing every rotten thing
he wanted and never worried about his future.

Until one morning when he woke up feeling very, very tired. He had spent the night being rotten with his alley cat friends. Now he could barely roll out of bed. Finally he got up and drifted toward the bathroom.

Suddenly, he cried out loud.
In the mirror he looked like a ghost.
He was so pale, he could almost see right through himself.

"Sarah!" he wailed. "Help me!"
Sarah came running to rescue Ralph.
"Oh, dear," she said when she saw him.
"You don't look well. We'd better get to the vet."

Ralph was afraid of the vet, but this time he was glad to go.
I hope she makes me drink awful-tasting medicine, Ralph thought.
Sarah always says the worse it tastes, the better I'll feel.

The vet examined Ralph. Then she had some bad news for Sarah.
"I've seen this before. Your cat has used up eight of his nine lives,"
she whispered. She pointed toward the Nine Lives Chart.
"Sadly, I believe his best days are behind him."

NINE LIVES CHART

1. OUCH!

2. Too Bad!

3. Triple Trouble

4. Not Good 4 You

5. Halfway to Cat Heaven

6. Risky Business

7. Time to Take It Easy

8. Stay Under the Covers

9. Next Stop: Cat Heaven
(Good Cats Only!)

Sarah was puzzled. "How could this happen?" she asked. She took such good care of Ralph. Just then Rotten Ralph read the chart. He fainted and fell to the floor.

Sarah picked him up.
Ralph groaned.
"Remember," warned the vet,
as Sarah carried Ralph out
the door, "he's down to his
last life. One more slip and
he'll be gone forever."

When they returned home Sarah gently stretched Ralph out on the couch. She sat next to him and patted his worried brow. When he felt better Sarah asked the big question that was on her mind. "Ralph," she said, "how did you lose so many lives?"

"The first life lost was when I was left behind at the circus," he said with a sniffle.
"They only fed me stale popcorn and rotten candied apples. That did me in."

"And I'll never forget the time Mr. Pierre caught me running wild in his Poodle Parlor," he moaned. "That was fun until he got me by the tail."

"Then there was the time you took me to school for show and tell," he recalled, shuddering. "I knocked over the red ant farm and the angry ants carried me away. They did not play nice."

Ralph thought back to his cousin
Percy's Christmas visit. Ralph had been very rotten to
Percy, so Percy had rolled a giant snowball off the roof.
It landed on Ralph's head.
"I don't think I deserved to lose a life over that."
Ralph sniffled again.

"What about that black cat you chased on Halloween?" Sarah asked as she wiped his eyes. Ralph whimpered. "That was a witch's cat and it turned me into a carved pumpkin."

And then he remembered his worst birthday ever.
Ralph wouldn't share his cake. So everyone played pin
the tail on the *cat* with him.

"That was definitely not a happy birthday," he said sadly.

Suddenly, he thought of sweet Petunia. He had brought a squished stinkbug to her Valentine's party. In return, she'd squished him like a bug. Ralph sighed. "Petunia was a lot tougher than I thought."

 But the worst was Mr. Fred. "He carried me kicking and screaming into the self-control room at his cat obedience school," Ralph remembered. "I was lucky to get out of there with just one lost life."

Sarah counted up the lost lives on her fingers. *That makes eight,* she thought. *And if those eight lives were his* best *days, his future does not look bright.* "Well, Ralph," she announced, "your rotten days are behind you. I'll protect you from here on out."

First, she made certain Ralph did not do anything to hurt himself. She dressed him like he was a little baby kitten. She spoonfed him in his old baby buggy.

When Ralph went to eat a mouse, Sarah had to taste it first. "It might be poisoned," she cautioned. She took a bite. "Disgusting," she announced. "But safe."

The more Ralph missed his old rotten life, the worse he felt.
He looked out the window. All his cat friends were climbing trees.
They were chasing squirrels. They were tiptoeing across laundry lines.
Sarah's gone too far, he thought.

The next morning Sarah got ready for school. "While I'm away I want you to eat your Vital Vitamins and drink your Anti-Germ Juice," she instructed. Rotten Ralph groaned. "It will kill me to sit inside all day and do nothing."

The moment Sarah was out the
door, Ralph took off his baby
clothes and leapt out a window.

"Life is not going to pass me by," he said.
He ran into the aquarium and grabbed the
electric eels. That shocked him back into action.

He dashed over to the carnival and took a seat in the
Cat-A-Pult. He was blasted all the way across town.
It felt good to have so much rotten fun.
Then he ran off looking for mean dogs to tease.

When Sarah came home, Ralph was missing.
"Oh, no," she cried. "I knew I shouldn't have
trusted him with his last life."
She called out his name. She searched everywhere.
She tacked up little posters of his picture.
But she could not find Ralph.

missing cat!

if seen, please
call Sarah!

LOST!

Have you
seen me?

call Sarah!

LOST!

Have you seen me?

Finally, as she walked back home she looked up at the stars.
They seemed to form an outline of a cat in the dark night sky.
"I only hope he *makes* it into cat heaven," she said, sniffing sadly.

But Ralph was not in cat heaven.
He was safely snoozing on the couch. Sarah was so surprised.
She jumped on him and gave him a big hug.
"Why you rotten cat!" she growled. "You almost sent *me* to cat heaven."
Don't do that, Ralph thought. *I only have one life left . . . and for you I've saved the best for last.*